A Shepherd's Gift

Mary Calhoun

ILLUSTRATED BY

Raúl Colón

To Sister Anne Michelle,
who asked me to tell a Christmas story,
and to Sister Faith, who encourages me
—M.C.

For three little shepherds:
Hunter, Kaeden, and Savannah
—R.C.

▆▆ H A R P E R C O L L I N S *P U B L I S H E R S*

Library of Congress Cataloging-in-Publication Data Calhoun, Mary. A shepherd's gift / Mary Calhoun ; illustrated by Raúl Colón.—1st ed. p. cm. Summary: While looking for his lost lamb, an orphaned shepherd boy meets Mary, Joseph, and newborn baby Jesus in a manger. ISBN 0-688-15176-0 — ISBN 0-688-15177-9 (lib. bdg.) 1. Jesus Christ—Nativity—Juvenile fiction. [1. Jesus Christ— Nativity—Fiction. 2. Shepherds—Fiction. 3. Orphans—Fiction.] I. Colón, Raúl, ill. PZ7.C1278 Sh 2001 [E]—dc21 00-32020 CIP AC
Typography by Matt Adamec 1 2 3 4 5 6 7 8 9 10 ❖ First Edition

Matthew's lamb cried for her mother. He held the lamb close. "I can't find her," he whispered.

He had searched up the hillside where the shepherds camped with their flocks. He had climbed down a rocky edge where a sheep could fall over. Not there.

The sheep and lamb were his, the pay for his work. Even though he was an orphan, the other shepherds were fair to him. Matthew had loved the lamb since she was born.

"Baaa!" She nibbled at his shirt, hungry.

The shepherd boy milked a ewe and soaked a rag in the bowl of milk. He dripped the milk into the lamb's mouth, then let her suck on the rag.

But she bleated "baaa!" again, letting go of the rag. The lamb scrambled to her feet and ran off to find her mother's milk.

"Come back!" Matthew chased after his lamb.

When he reached for her, she darted aside and dashed down the hill. Matthew tripped on a rock and tumbled after her to the bottom.

They were on the edge of a town. He had seen people traveling

there all day. It was getting dark, and torches blazed in the streets.

The lamb stopped to sniff the air, and Matthew nearly caught her.

Then she was off again, running to a stable dug into the hillside.

The boy followed her inside. By the dim light of an oil lamp he could see several kinds of animals, some sleeping, some feeding at troughs. And there was his lamb nuzzled up to her mother.

"Aha!" Matthew laughed. "Smart girl, you found her!" He patted the lamb's back. Now he could lead both his sheep back to the shepherds' camp.

"Welcome," came a voice in the dimness.

"My lamb found her mother!" Quickly Matthew claimed them.

"Yes, the lost sheep came to us." The man's voice was kind.

Farther inside Matthew saw a young woman lying against a roll of cloaks. She was nursing a small baby. Nearby was a bundle of the couple's belongings.

"Do you live here?" Matthew asked.

"We are travelers," said the man.

The mother gave Matthew a soft smile as she said, "The inn was crowded with people. We were led to this quiet place for our son to be born."

"The animals make it warm," the man added.

Matthew noticed that a donkey's head was near the mother's shoulder, as if he were watching over her and the baby. Hens clucked sleepily, *cuk-cuk*.

Seeing this family, Matthew suddenly missed his mother

and father, whom he could barely remember.

"Can I help you here?" he asked,

wanting to be a part of this

gentle family, if only for

a little while.

The man nodded. "Ah, yes."

He handed Matthew a jug.

"It would be good

if you could

fetch more

water."

Matthew took the jug to the inn. The bright room was filled with

noise and people. He was glad to leave there and return to the stable.

In the yellow lamplight he saw the mother give her baby to the man. Their faces glowed with happiness.

Nursing lamb, quiet donkey—the stable was a place of peace. It made a safe shelter for the newborn child.

The baby fit snugly in the man's big hands. The little one was wrapped in a cloth, and only his tiny head showed.

The man laid him on a bed of straw in a feeding trough. Then he took a cloak from the roll under the mother's shoulders and spread it over her.

Matthew knelt at the trough to look at the baby. Coming near, he was amazed at the feeling of peace that filled him as he watched the sleeping infant.

Then the baby yawned, and the boy saw his little pink tongue. The baby closed his lips and worked them in a sucking movement. Opening his mouth again, he breathed a milky bubble onto his lips. It glowed golden in the soft light.

Matthew whispered, "Oh, my sweet!"

The baby opened his eyes and gazed at Matthew with eyes as bright as stars. The boy gasped. It was as if the baby knew him. Matthew clasped his hands in delight, smiling at the child.

"What is his name?" he asked.

The mother said, "His name is Jesus."

The baby's eyes closed again in sleep.

Matthew's lamb bleated, and the shepherd boy rose to his feet.

"The straw might scratch his skin," he told the man. "Keep my

sheep. You can shear her wool, and Jesus can lie on the soft fleece."

"Too fine a gift!" the man protested.

But the mother said, "Thank you, friend."

In his sleep, the baby drew a deeper breath.

The man took bread from their pack. "Will you eat with us?"

"No, I must go back to the sheep camp."

Matthew petted his lamb between the ears. She would need to stay with her mother, but he was happy to give the lamb too. Much as he loved her, he loved the baby more.

He looked at Jesus as he slept and said, "I'll never forget you."

As Matthew climbed the hillside, a growing light shone on his way. He thought he heard voices. They seemed to be singing about that wonderful child who knew him, an ordinary shepherd.